JACK B. NINJA

by TIM McCANNA • illustrated by STEPHEN SAVAGE

ORCHARD BOOKS • NEW YORK • AN IMPRINT OF SCHOLASTIC INC.

For Caryn Wiseman, my ninja agent — T. M.

For Eli — S. S.

Text copyright © 2018 by Tim McCanna
Illustrations copyright © 2018 by Stephen Savage

Library of Congress Cataloging-in-Publication Data available

ISBN 978-0-545-91728-5

10 9 8 7 6 5 4 3 2 1   18 19 20 21 22   Printed in China 38   First edition, July 2018

The text type was set in Linotype Spitz Book. The display type was hand-lettered by the artist. Book design by Stephen Savage and David Saylor

Jack B. Ninja! Jack, be quick!
Jack, jump over the bamboo stick!

Secret mission starts tonight.
Hide in shadow, out of sight.

Jack B. Ninja, way up high,
watches as the guards go by.
Waits until the coast is clear.
Never shows a hint of fear.

Jack B. Ninja keeps his cool.

Dips into the garden pool.

Takes a breath, then dives below.

Spots a tunnel. Go, Jack, go!

Jack B. Ninja, bold and brave,
breaks into a bandit cave.
Tiptoes, searching through the dark.
Makes no sound and leaves no mark.

Jack B. Ninja, on his quest,
finds the stolen treasure chest!

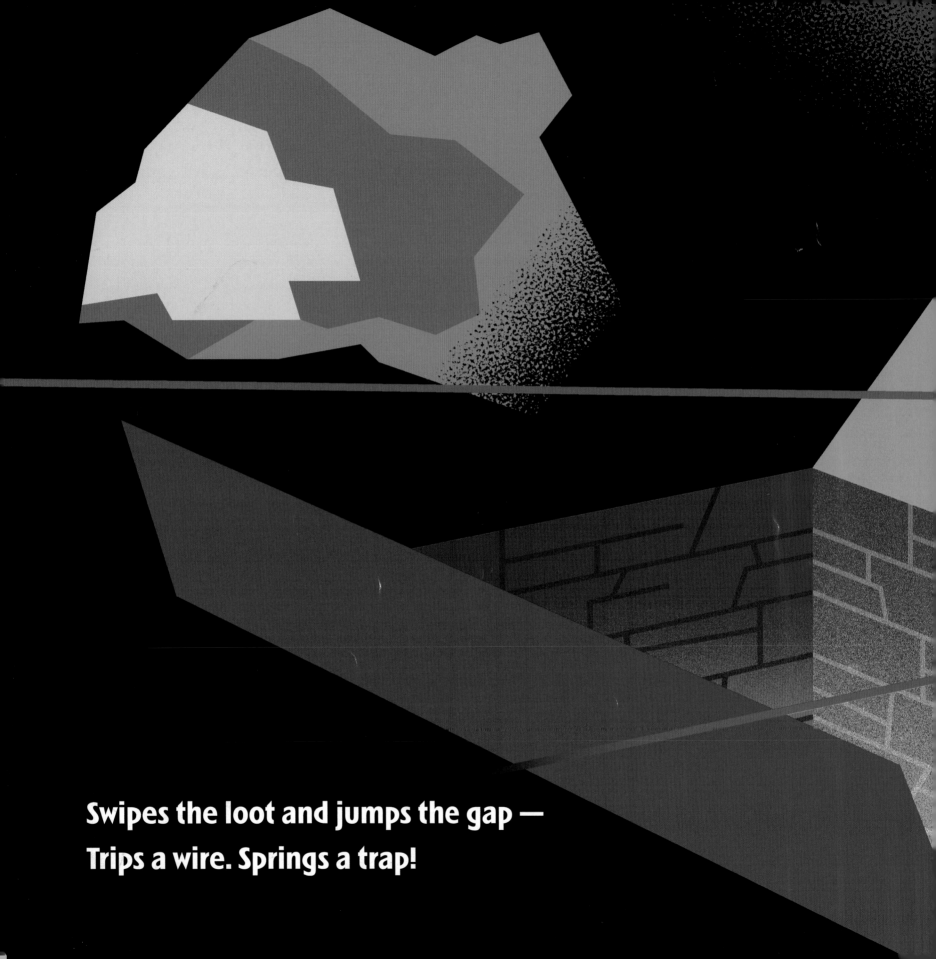

Swipes the loot and jumps the gap —
Trips a wire. Springs a trap!

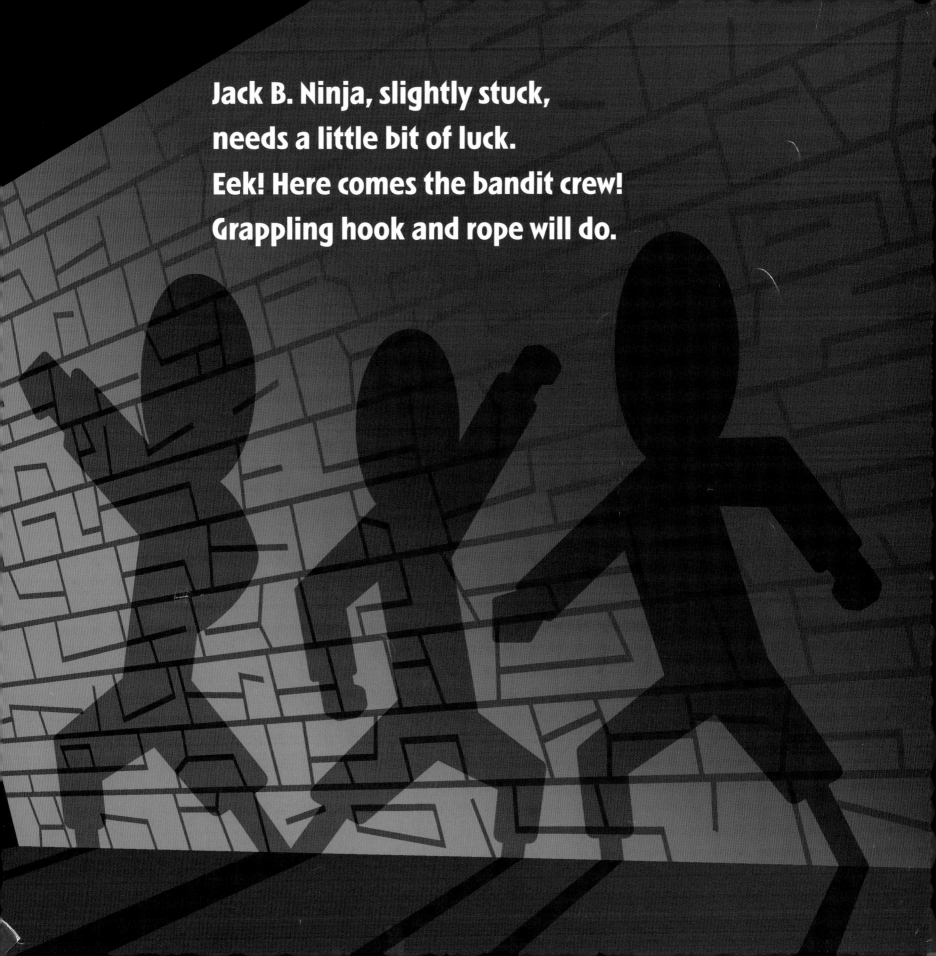

Jack B. Ninja, slightly stuck,
needs a little bit of luck.
Eek! Here comes the bandit crew!
Grappling hook and rope will do.

Jack B. Ninja must work fast.
Dodges! Leaps! Escapes at last!

Brings the prize to Ninja Master.
"Could have been a little faster."

"Jack B. Ninja, job well done,"
says the Master to his son.
"Take a look around for me."
Jack obeys. What does he see?

Jack B. Ninja jumps with fright.
"Look out, bandits! Now we fight!"

"Jack, don't worry!" Mama cries.
"We're your family in disguise!"

Jack B. Ninja hugs each one.
"Thank you for the ninja fun!"
"Time for cake!" they clap and shout.
"Light the candles! Blow them out!"

Jack B. Ninja flips and kicks.
Cartwheels over the candlesticks.
All the ninjas dance and cheer.
Then, like that, they —